Hard Hart

A Bi Awakening Steamy MM Short Story

(First Time for Everything Series)

By B.T. Haiyes

Table of Contents

Chapter 1

JAMES

The car revved so loud, I gritted my teeth as the sound of the engine began to reach ear-splitting levels.

"I get it!," I yelled, barely able to hear my own voice over the volume of the engine. Slapping the hood of the car, the overheated metal nearly scalded my palm, as I tried to capture Tony's attention.

Tony, meanwhile, was hunched over the wheel of the car, revving the engine for all it was worth.

Still, the firm thud's from my hand slapping the hood did the trick as Tony lifted his gaze up from the wheel.

"What?" Tony yelled back, although I could barely make out the word.

I mimed a *cutting* action across my neck with one hand, and pointed at the car bonnet with the other. "Switch it off!"

Tony, the manager of the auto repair shop, where I'd been working for the past year, finally got the hint, and cut the engine.

The silence that followed was blissful, although it was soon broken by Tony's harried voice. "So, what do you think it is? Why is it sounding like that?" Tony asked as he collapsed back into the car seat.

I absentmindedly rubbed the back of my neck. The rough burn scars that marred the skin on my neck, always seemed to itch whenever I got even a little frustrated.

Too late I remembered the greasy car oil smeared on my palms, and dropped my hand from my neck. I sighed. "Look," I reached around to snatch a dirty rag from my back pocket. "Leave the car here with me. I'll take a further look at it," I said as I wiped the grease off my palm and neck, "but it's going to take a bit of time." I turned to wave a hand around the small auto shop we were in, indicating the three other cars that I still had to work on. "With other customers ahead in the queue, it'll be a while before I can get to it."

Tony nodded quickly, a little too quickly for me to think he'd actually heard a word I'd said. And the next sentence out of his mouth proved me right.

"Yeah, yeah, so here's the thing. I told my wife I would fix this car for her," Tony looked shamefaced as he continued with a grimace, "and that was around a couple weeks ago."

I gave him a slow exasperated shake of my head. "The car's been here the whole time," I said as I wafted away exhaust fumes that thickened the air around us. "Why didn't you say anything?"

Tony was your all-round family man, and he talked about his wife all the time. He spoke of her as though she'd plucked the stars from the sky. Yet, this wasn't the first time he'd forgotten to tell me about a car he'd needed fixed on a rush order.

"I know, I know," my boss nodded his head in agreement. "So do you think you can fix it?"

I scratched the side of my chin, giving it a little thought. "From the sound of that engine, I figure the throttle is stuck maybe? Possibly some trouble with the mass airflow sensor..." I let my voice fade away into silence for a moment.

Noticing the blank look on Tony's face, I knew he had no clue what I was talking about. Tony's a good manager, but a mechanic, he was not.

He'd taken over the shop a few weeks before he'd hired me. And he'd told me that he thought the shop would be a great way to stay busy after retiring as an accountant.

Tony did the books, and dealt with the customers. And he needed a mechanic who'd be happy to work in a one-man shop.

And I needed a job that'd let me keep my head down, and away from people. So, working in the back of an auto shop, as the sole mechanic, let me do that.

Tony's eyes began to take on a pleading glint. I sighed again. Tony let me work at my own pace more often than not. So, the least I could do is take on this last-minute rush job.

"Sure," I finally conceded, but made a 'calm-down' motion at the excited look of relief on Tony's face. "But I am not making any promises. I was only guessing at what could be the problem."

"Of course, of course," Tony agreed a little too quickly, his attention already away from me and down towards the phone he'd plucked out of his pocket. I gave him a quizzical eye as he tapped in a telephone number he clearly knew by heart.

"Let me just tell my wife I've got it all sorted out," Tony said with a grin, cellphone already by his ear.

I took a breath, ready to remind him that I couldn't guarantee I'd get the car fixed any time soon, when the high pitched 'ding' of the front desk service bell rang.

Both Tony and I turned towards the small desk at the front of the shop. And there stood a man who waved at us with a wordless greeting.

I eyed the newcomer, judging him with a long look, taking in his harried features and his ruffled blond hair.

Tony yelled out to the man. "Yeah, we'll be right with you!" then quickly lowered his voice as he spoke into the phone that he still held to his ear. "Honey, good news! About the car, James is on it like I promised." Tony then paused, turning the cellphone away from his mouth as he whispered to me, "I'm gonna need you to take this customer. I'll be right back out in a moment."

"Woah, wait a minute..."

Before I could complete my sentence, Tony paced towards his office out the back, moving sprightly for a man in his sixties, as he left me alone to deal with the new customer.

I let loose a frustrated breath, as I took in the newcomers easy manner. And I gave him a careful once over as I watched him nonchalantly glancing around the auto-shop.

This was the bit I hated. My deal with Tony was that I always stayed with the cars, and he handled the desk. But, every now and then, Tony liked to forget just how bad I was with clients.

I can deal with car engines. It was the people who drove them that I couldn't handle... *not anymore, not for a long while.*

It had been over 2 years since second degree burns had charred my skin. And the pain of the memory of my former life as a firefighter pricked the back of my mind.

It was with that thought that I lifted up the hood of my grease-stained hoodie, hating how I felt the need to hide my scars.

As I approached the customer, I couldn't help but notice his impossibly green eyes. But, I caught myself staring when I noticed he was waiting for me to speak.

Clearing my throat, I hunched my shoulders a little. "So, what do you need?"

I didn't mean to be so curt. But hey, I don't like people, so you get what you get.

"Um, well," the man began, as he ran a hand through his dirty blond hair, "my car completely gave out on me." He then jutted a thumb behind him, and I looked over his shoulder and noticed his car parked in the shop driveway.

Just by eyeballing the thing, I could see it was on its last shaky legs. It's front bumper was hanging on by a thread. Literally. And the windscreen wipers had clearly seen better days—years even.

And was that side mirror duct taped on?

I gave the car a dubious look, before turning my attention back to the man who'd continued speaking. I hadn't even caught most of what he'd said, because I was so surprised the car had even made it this far.

"...and that's when I figured I would walk it here the rest of the way," he babbled on as I fixed my doubtful gaze on his apologetic one. "And you're wondering how the car made it here, right?" the man let loose a small chuckle, clearly reading the skepticism evident on my face. "Well, I pushed it the last quarter mile," he concluded with a helpless shrug.

I waited for him to continue, but I guess he was all out of explanations, so I prepared to give him the bad news. "Look, I gotta tell you..." I let my voice drift off with a meaningful shake of my head, but stopped when the man cut in.

"Dylan."

"What?" I asked, confused, pausing as Dylan repeated his name.

"The name's Dylan Reed," he said, reaching out a hand which I took. His grip was firm and confident, the grip of a man who—unroadworthy car aside—knew what he was about.

That's when I finally gave Dylan a good once over. I wasn't quite an old man myself at the ripe age of 27, but I figured Dylan must've been in his early twenties.

At first glance, I'd dismissed him as just another college kid. But, his slender build was more defined than I'd otherwise noticed.

And, Dylan's green eyes—paired with the small quirk of his lips—carried a friendly twinkle about them that disarmed me.

"James Hart," I offered my name cautiously, to which Dylan gave me a curt nod, letting go of my hand as he continued.

"I know how my car looks. But I need it to keep going for at least a few more weeks."

I turned to eye the vehicle again. "Look, nothing short of the hand of God is going to keep your ride going, my friend."

"Are you sure?" Dylan asked, a hint of hope coloring his voice, "how much would it cost to take a look at it?"

"Honestly, I'd be willing to pay **you** not to get back in that thing."

Dylan let loose a laugh at my reply, a warm sound accompanied by an easy smile.

I was starting to notice a lot more about Dylan now. His tight white t-shirt and well-fitted jeans did nothing to hide what was clearly a firm but slender physique underneath his clothes.

Dylan's arms weren't flexed, but the extra short sleeves of his top let him display his clearly athletic arms. His shirt was half a size too small. Still I snuck a look at the tightly packed abs stretching against the white fabric of his tee.

I'd lived a life long enough to have had my share of sexual fumbles with men and women, something I'd never sought to hide. So, I gave Dylan's body silent appreciation.

Dylan moved to stand beside me, as though he too were looking at his car for the first time. That was when I noticed that he came up a few inches short of my own six foot four inch frame.

I folded my arms, tilting my head as I turned my attention back to Dylan's car. "How soon do you need it up and running?"

Chapter 2

DYLAN

Sweet baby Jesus, this guy was tall.

I looked up at James, and tried to hide my awe at his immense build. At a touch under six foot nothing, I was hardly short. But, standing next to this man, I felt I'd shrunk a few inches in his presence.

James must have had half a foot on me, his broad shoulders emphasizing his physique. That baggy hoodie he wore up over his head, couldn't hide the fact that this man must have been a running back in a past life.

I began to wonder if that was true. Maybe he was a former college football star turned mechanic. Or maybe he simply had a really great workout regime, and power lifted cars in his downtime.

With his arms crossed, I noticed how his biceps still bulged through his thin-cotton hoodie. But they didn't even compare to his forearms.

With his sleeves rolled up, I could clearly see he'd developed them through sheer hard work. Those weren't the forearms of a body builder. They were the incredibly buff forearms of a man who physically worked hard for a living. And, the large intricately defined lion face tattoos visible on each arm, only added to the hardened appearance of him.

But, when I looked into his eyes, they were friendly. Despite his almost disinterested monotone voice, James' eyes held a warmth that surprised me.

I startled, when James said my name, interrupting my train of thought. "Um, come again?" I asked, a little too meekly for my liking, but I had just been caught gaping at a guy who looked like he could snap me in half for fun.

"I said, how soon you need the car by?" He repeated, as he pinned me with those impossible-to-read blue eyes.

I nodded and gave him a small shrug to distract from my blatant staring. I then switched my gaze back onto my battered mode of transport. Rubbing the rough stubble on my chin, I thought back to earlier, when I'd had to push the car the last few blocks to the auto-shop.

My car has been with me for nearly three years. She was already long in the tooth when I got her, but I didn't care. All that mattered was that I had a car, and I no longer needed to use the unreliable transport system.

But now, I was starting to realize that this auto-shop could very well be my vehicles final resting place.

"As soon as you can, but ideally within the next week." I wandered over to the drivers side of my vehicle. "Can't go too long without my chick magnet," I said mournfully as I patted the bonnet of the car.

To my surprise, James laughed, a genuine rumble of sound, one that sent a small—and unexpected—thrill through me.

What the hell was that? I chastised myself, not understanding the tingle of excitement that I felt at the sound of his voice.

"Look," James began, as he made his way over to me. He gave me a mock serious look as he placed a large palm on my shoulder. "I'm not gonna lie. If the ladies are flocking to you, it is not because of this car."

I felt the beginnings of a small blush creep up the side of my face. I didn't get compliments much, from men **or** from women, and I had no idea what to say in reply.

Thankfully, James continued talking before I put my foot in my mouth.

"Here's what I'll do." James dropped his warm hand from my shoulder, moving around to pop the hood of the car. "I'll take a look at it for free. We usually charge $100 for a full assessment, but don't worry about that. If there's anything wrong, which there will be," James stated with a meaningful look, before returning his attention to the engine, "I'll let you know how much you can expect to pay to fix it."

Warmed by his generosity, I wanted to pay James back in someway. "That would be great, thanks! Hey, I work at a bar part time a few blocks down from here," I began rambling, bringing his attention back to me. "I work there a few hours every evening. Come on over, and the first two rounds of drinks are on me."

James, once again, fixed me with that inscrutable stare, and I watched as he raised his hand to rub his neck. The movement drew my attention to what appeared to be scars on the side of his neck, hidden underneath his hoodie.

He must have noticed me noticing, because he quickly dropped his hand with a small shake of his head. "I'm not really into the whole nightclub scene."

I shook my head quickly. "It's not a nightclub. It's just a small bar, real friendly, everyones chill." I paused, remembering one or two regular patrons that I always found a handful, when they had one too many drinks. "Well, mostly everyones chill," I said, rushing into the next sentence, "but, hey, to sweeten the deal, the first three—*yes three!*—rounds are on me. What do you say?"

Chapter 3

JAMES

I stood outside a rough-looking bar, staring up at it's faded sign.

I was still a little surprised at myself at having taken Dylan up on his offer on a drink...or three. But, there was something about Dylan's openness that made me want to take a chance on turning up.

The Tailback, as the red sign above the entryway read, looked like a real dive. The bar's windows gleamed, clearly cleaned with care. But, the rest of the brickwork on the front of the establishment was less well cared for.

There was graffiti marring sections of the front wall, and the brickwork was chipped. Even the steps leading into the place had an ankle-breaking dip in the middle of them. And those steps themselves looked as though they'd been worn down by the pitter-patter of endless drunken feet.

I let loose a short breath when my hands itched. They twitched as I fought the impulse to rub the injury roughened skin on the side of my neck. But I resisted.

'May as well get this over with,' I thought to myself.

As I opened the door to the bar and stepped inside, I could feel the heat of the afternoon sun disappear behind me as I entered the air-conditioned establishment.

From the outside, this place didn't look all that classy. But, inside, the bar was surprisingly nice.

Outside, the owner had clearly made no effort to make the place inviting. However, inside the bar was a very different matter.

I let my eyes adjust to the dimmed lighting, as I scanned the room.

Everything, from the stools to the bar to the tables, were made from what look like well-aged reclaimed wood.

It felt like I'd entered an Old English pub. Or, at the very least, as though I'd stepped onto the set of a Hollywood movie about Elves and Orcs.

There was almost no one in here to appreciate it though. Which I could understand, what with it still being a little too early for drinking.

I figured the bar would be half empty when I arrived here at 2pm. *OK, fine, I'd hoped it would be completely empty.*

And, glancing around the room, taking in the musky scent of Cedar wood and whiskey, I noticed only one other patron in the premise. Some guy, that I could barely make out in the dim lighting, was slumped over a table in the corner.

I shrugged off my curiosity about him. *'I'm here for Dylan'.* I paused at that thought. *'No,'* I corrected myself, *'I am here for the free drinks from Dylan. Right?'*

As I moved towards the bar, I saw that no-one appeared to be manning it. But, I did hear movement and soft chatter coming from an open side door at the end of the bar.

As I sat down heavily on one of the stools, I made sure to make plenty of noise as I did.

A few seconds later, Dylan popped his head around the side door, and took a peak at me. And, I could have sworn, his eyes actually lit up.

"Hey, you came," Dylan said enthusiastically, popping his head back around the side door before I had a chance to answer. "I gotta get back to the bar," I heard him yell over to someone behind him, before rushing back out again with a kitchen towel in hand.

"Sorry about that," Dylan said, as he hurried to move behind the bar. "I honestly thought you weren't gonna take me up on my offer," he continued, with an easy smile that I fought hard not to return.

Damn, this guy was getting to me, and I couldn't figure out why.

"Yeah, well," I began gruffly with a shrug, "it's the middle of the afternoon, and the garage is quiet right now".

That was a lie, of course. I was swamped with a back log of cars that needed work. Still, Dylan didn't know that.

"Yeah. I get you," Dylan said as he swept a hand to indicate the empty drinking hole. There was no chatter, save for the sound of the small TV screen set up at the far end of the bar. "It's usually bustling after 6pm, but not much happening during the day."

"Sure," I said with a noncommittal reply. It's been so long since I'd talked to another human being about something other than cars. And I felt lost as to how to keep the conversation going.

So, I fell back onto old habits. "Well, your car should be done in a few more days, tops."

Dylan waved it off. "That's okay, I mean sure, I'm not happy to be taking the bus right now. But, you get to it when you get to it. Dude, you're really helping me out." I nodded as Dylan jutted a thumb over his shoulder, indicating the side door. "Maria—she's the owner of this place by the way—she pays well. But," Dylan shrugged, "it's hard to get extra shifts here when it's been so quiet lately. So, money saved is as good as money earned for me right now."

I nodded wordlessly, and I noticed how Dylan shifted from one foot to the other at my lack of a reply. I racked my brain trying to think of something—anything—to fill the lull in conversation. But, once again, Dylan seemed to take up the chit-chat mantel for both of us.

"So, what can I get you?" Dylan spread his arms to indicate the selection of whiskeys and gins lining the bar behind him. "Any drink you want, it's on the house. Just like I promised," he said with a cheeky grin.

My mouth quirked at that, in a way that felt like the first smile I'd cracked in a while. "Well, actually, you promised me three drinks," I lifted my hand, three fingers wriggling in front of my face. "And, I'm not a whiskey kind of guy. I'm all about All American beer."

"Of course," Dylan said, already drawing me a beer from the tap, "the first of three beers coming up."

The silence settled between us again, but this time it was an easy one. It was one filled with the promise of camaraderie, and I felt myself relax. So much so, I tugged my hoodie off my head, stretching my neck a little, shrugging off the stiffness.

Dylan finished pouring my drink, holding my gaze for a long moment with a warm smile as he handed it to me. Just as I began to think he was noticing my scars, Dylan spoke. "I figured you would have had a buzz crop hairstyle. It looks good on you."

I reached up and run my hand over my short cropped hair. "Yeah I know. I used to grow it out like yours, but I guess I didn't have the hair products for it," I said with a smirk.

Dylan laughed, enjoying my little jibe at his highly stylized hair. His hair stood up every which fashionable way, looking like it was being kept in place by a ridiculous amount of gel.

"What can I say. It gets me the ladies. Gotta keep it looking good."

"I thought it was your car that got you the ladies. Already giving up on your chick magnet?" I said as I went to grab a handful of peanuts from the complimentary bowl atop the bar.

Dylan startled me when he quickly placed his hand on top of mine. I stopped mid-movement, peanuts still clutched in my grasp, as I reveled in the warmth of Dylan's palm.

I gave him a questioning look as we stayed there like that for a moment. And looking into Dylan's eyes, I felt I saw the same curious questioning look staring right back at me.

I didn't move, waiting for Dylan to say something. But, at the same time, I selfishly hoped he wouldn't say a word, just so that I would have an excuse for him to keep touching me.

'God damn it', I thought to myself, *is this what my old therapist meant by me being touch-starved?*.

Thoughts of my mandatory fire service therapy session, (from a couple years back), quickly came and went, when Dylan cleared his throat.

I watched as Dylan snatched his hand back, and I felt disappointment at the loss of its warmth.

"Don't eat the peanuts," Dylan mumbled, nervously tucking his hands in his pockets. "I mean, don't take the peanuts. I didn't want you to grab the...wait, let me start again," Dylan rambled as he fumbled for words. I tried not to smile as he did so. "Those peanuts are not meant for human consumption. *Seriously*." Dylan wrinkled his nose in disgust at the peanut bowl. And I quickly dropped the peanuts, wiping my hand on the side of my jeans.

"Gotcha," I replied.

Chapter 4

DYLAN

I could have slapped myself for over-reacting to a mere touch.

'*Get it together Dylan*', I scolded myself, turning away to wipe down the bar.

An awkward silence fell between James and myself, as I tried to get our conversation back on track.

"Yeah, anyway," I began, as I kept my eyes averted. At this precise moment, I found that spot on the bar the most intriguing thing in the world. "I was gonna throw those out today." As I spoke, I could feel heat coloring my cheeks, like some silly kid with a crush.

'*This is ridiculous!*' I chastised myself again. What was it about this guy that made me feel...***things***. Things I'd only ever felt for women before.

'*Sure, he's a good looking guy*', I thought to myself as the silence stretched. I risked a sneak peek, half-hoping James had turned away to watch the TV.

To my surprise and embarrassment, I found James staring right back, his strikingly blue eyes twinkling in amusement over the rim of his beer glass.

Seems like he'd never turned his attention from me the entire time.

'*Fuck*'.

I straightened, and met his stare as he slowly sipped his beer. Then a thought thankfully came to mind. "So, you like cars then?"

I stifled a groan, recognizing that it wasn't the best conversation starter. But, I was desperate to get things flowing again with this otherwise tight-lipped man.

James chuckled, raising a hand to thoughtfully rub his beard. "It keeps me busy, and pays the rent."

I flipped the kitchen towel over my shoulder and then leaned forward, resting my hands on the bar. "You've always been a mechanic?"

"You've always been a bartender?" James replied smartly, but not unkindly, as he leaned a little forward.

I could feel a tension and an intimacy in the move, one that I recognized. And why was that? Well, because I'd used that exact move myself on any girl I tried to hit on.

'Wait, is James flirting with me?'

"Nah," I replied, "I'm a science post-grad. I'm just doing this bar tending job to keep myself going, while I wait to see if my sponsorship applications go through." I paused, eyebrow quirked. "And, of course, I bar tend for the good company."

I had no idea why I was flirting back. I mean, sure, it felt good to be wanted. It's rare that guys like me get hit on. I was no slouch in the looks department, I'll admit that. But women weren't exactly beating down my door for a little action.

Neither were men, come to think of it.

So, it felt good to be wanted by someone I felt comfortable with. I waved away the thought. *'This is a man crush,'* I told myself. *'It's just misplaced admiration.'*

I looked on, curious, when James sighed as he set his half-drunk beer glass down. "I haven't always been a mechanic."

He reached up to rub the side of his neck, touching the noticeable scars that criss-crossed his skin. Those scars told a story, one I was dying to hear. Still, I was waiting for James to tell me when he was ready.

"Yeah?" I nudged, eager to learn more.

"Yeah," James echoed, as he gave me a wry smile. "I used to be a firefighter for a few years." James nodded at my raised eyebrows. "Surprised?"

"A little," I admitted with a shrug. "I figured you for an ex-college football player."

James let loose a short bark of a laugh. "Really?" He shook his head with a low chuckle, "That game is not my speed. I'm more of a baseball kinda guy."

"Not into whiskey, not into football," I began to tick off what I'd learned about James so far. "So, beer," I raised a finger, "cars," I raised a second finger, "and baseball." I raised a third finger, before curling my hand into a finger gun, and gestured at James playfully. "Gotcha," I said, and then noticed James glass was almost empty. "Shall I fill you up again?"

Before he could reply, our conversation was interrupted by a slurred growl. "You can fill *my* glass up first."

Both James and I turned to notice that the man slumped in the corner table had dragged himself to the bar. He now sat a couple seats down from James.

I blew out a frustrated breath. "Damn it Mack," I began, as I wandered over to him. "You know you're cut off." I took Mack's empty shot glass and put it in the sink behind me.

"You don't get to cut me off," Mack groused, before raising his voice. "Where is Maria, where is she. You want me to tell your boss you cut me off?"

I shook my head. "She was the one who cut you off. And you being cut off? That hasn't changed in the last hour. So, go home. You look wrecked," I said, as I moved my way around to the front of the bar.

Wrecked was putting it politely. Mack looked like a eleven car pile up, all rolled up into the body of a broken man. His bloodshot eyes sat sunken in amongst the sickly pallor of his skin. And his greasy messy hair shaded his eyes, as he sneered at me.

"Go get Maria. Get her to tell me that to my face." I could hear an edge in Mack's voice that clearly signaled he was gearing up to be trouble again.

Mack was here everyday, drinking his ample weight in beer. He was good for business, and bad for business, as Maria liked to say.

That's because this guy had a nasty streak in him, something that tended to come through at around shot number four.

At that point, Maria would always tell me to just cut Mack off. But, this afternoon, Mack wasn't having any of it.

I lightly grasped his shoulder. "Come on, don't make me..." I began, but my voice faded as Mack stood up to face me down.

'OK,' I thought as Mack loomed over me. 'This is new'.

This wasn't the first time I'd tossed Mack out of the bar. Still, all those times, he'd always eventually gone of his own accord. Sure, he'd be complaining the whole time, but he'd make his own way out all the same.

But, this was the first time Mack looked like he was gearing up to fight back.

I dropped my hand from his shoulder. "It's for your own good," I started, trying to reason with him. But Mack pointed a finger in my face that made me pause.

"What? You want me out of here, so you can spend time alone with your boyfriend?" Mack sneered, disgust coloring his every word.

I did a double take. 'What?' I thought.

"What?" I said out loud, dumbfounded.

Mack jutted a thumb over at James, who continued to watch calmly as I tried to handle this.

Feeling a little ashamed at not being able to deal with Mack, I puffed up my chest.

So what if Mack had 40 pounds on me (and not all of it was beer gut). I wasn't a fighter—God knows I'd lost enough fights at high school to prove that point—but I wasn't going to back down either.

Still, I'd seen enough bar fights to know that most of it was just posturing. Simply guys trying to sooth their ego, when alcohol wasn't doing the job.

I raised my palms up, placating, "look, go home and sober up..." I started again. But this time, instead of a pointed finger, I watched as Mack's fist hurtled towards my face.

It took a couple seconds, but pain soon ballooned on my cheek, as the sharp sting of the rings on Mack's fist, sliced open my skin.

Chapter 5

JAMES

I saw red. Literally and figuratively.

Seeing the fresh line of blood on Dylan's cheek, I swiftly moved into action.

At first I was going to wait things out, and let Dylan hold his own. But, that all changed once this Mack guy decided to get violent.

Standing up, I grabbed Mack by the scruff of his shirt. And, in one move, I yanked him away from Dylan.

I'd clearly caught him by surprise...guess Mack didn't think I'd jump in.

But he was wrong.

"Who the hell do you think you are!" Mack slurred at me. But, I wasn't intimidated by his angry glare. I simply straightened, planting my feet as I readied for his attack.

Mack moved fast for a man who looked in his early forties. And that speed sat at odds with his inebriated state. It were as though lashing out at Dylan, had sobered Mack up.

Clearly, Mack could fight, even through the haze of hard liquor.

I'd known plenty of people that could function well when drunk. Hell, I'd worked with many a firefighter who hit the bottle hard after a shift, just to keep the pain of the day at bay.

And I also remembered how they could still keep up with the best of us, the very next shift.

But, I'd never been one for hard drinking. Not before, during, or even after, the fire blaze that had marred my skin.

Either way, it didn't matter. I'd faced enough angry people, back on the job at the fire department, (and off the job too), to handle myself.

Usually, the most violent were the people who felt the most helpless, fighting tooth and nail to run back into a burning building to save loved ones. And each time it happened, I would face down their anger and parry away their swinging fists.

The sensible ones would do a double take at my 6' 4" frame, and immediately cool down after their first hit. But, in extreme cases, I'd have no choice but to put them flat on their ass.

And it seemed like I was going to have to do the latter here once again.

I let Mack throw the first punch, letting him make contact. I could see he was putting his entire body behind it, as I braced myself.

Yet, the impact barely turned my head, and I easily absorbed the hit. My mouth quirked up when I saw how this made Mack hesitate. And his eyes lit up with a flicker of recognition at the knowledge that I was more than he could handle.

Still, I waited for him to either back down or to back away. Either outcome would be fine by me. But, now that adrenalin charged through my body, a small part of me wanted him to try and hit me again.

I wanted him to pay for laying a hand on Dylan. I barely knew the guy, but what I had learned of Dylan so far made me sure of one thing…he did ***not*** deserve to get his face cut open by some arrogant asshole.

'Come on, you prick', I thought to myself, as I stared Mack down, *'what else you got'.*

Mack did not disappoint. I watched as he shifted his hips, putting everything behind his swing. This time though, I moved to parry his attempt at a punch, raising my arm to block his.

This left him wide open, his gut an easy target for my fist.

I threw a punch dead center at his solar plexus, only giving the swing half the power that I was capable of.

I wanted him down, not out.

Once my fist connected, Mack let loose a pained gasp of air. Yet, before he had time to recover, I grasped his arm and side-stepped, twisting his outstretched arm up and away from me.

In a single move, I'd given myself the space I needed in order to throw an uppercut dead-center to his chin.

My knuckles made direct contact, snapping his head back with enough power to make Mack rock back against the bar.

I took half a step back as I eyed him carefully, waiting to see if the spark of animosity had left him.

I stood stock still, weight balanced on the balls of my feet, as Mack warily eyed me. He said nothing as I watched him grab his bruised and bristled chin, rubbing away at the hurt I'd put on him.

'Good', I thought, 'maybe now he'll listen to sense'.

"Dylan told you to leave," I said out loud, giving Mack an even glare. "I suggest you do that."

I stayed alert as Mack righted himself slowly, a low curse on his breath. Still, he didn't hang around, moving quickly to slink out of the bar, and into the street, without another word.

I tracked him as he left, carefully keeping myself between him and Dylan, who was now stood behind me.

And after the door closed behind Mack, I gave myself a few seconds to compose myself before I turned to face Dylan.

I found Dylan staring right back at me, his face filled with what looked like awe. And I wasn't quite sure what to do with it.

"You OK?" I asked him, discomfort turning into concern, as my attention was grabbed by the cut on his cheek. My fingers flexed, desperate to fix his injury, and wanting to sooth away the pain.

But, more than that, my fire fighter first aid training kicked in. At first glance, the cut looked bad. But, I wouldn't know either way until I cleaned it.

I indicated at Dylan's injury. "We're going to need to check that and fix it up," I said, just as a small round of applause began in the bar. And shaken out of my intense focus on Dylan, I took in the room.

It seemed that a few patrons had entered the bar since I'd arrived. Yet, I'd been so absorbed with my earlier conversation with Dylan, I hadn't noticed them come in.

However, one particular person stood out. A woman was leaning against the side door, clapping the loudest, a broad smile on her face. She looked to be in her fifties, a pen tucked behind her ear, almost hidden amongst her big salt and pepper hairdo.

She made her way over to me, a hand outstretched. "Well done! I've been wanting to do that to Mack for a while," she said. I grasped her hand to shake it, and she took my palm in both of her own. "You looking for a job in security? We could use a bit of muscle in here."

"Um...ouch?" Dylan said, his awe struck face now taking on a comical look of hurt. "I was handling Mack. I was just softening him up so James could take him out."

Maria hummed in agreement, but the tone of it made me think she wasn't quite convinced by Dylan's protestations. "Of course, honey," she said, looking bemused, "never had a doubt."

Maria was still shaking my hand when I looked over at Dylan and widened my eyes, imploring him for help.

Noticing my plea, Dylan stepped in. "James, meet my boss Maria. Maria, meet my friend James," Dylan said with a warmth that made me smile. I gave him a short nod, and returned my attention back to Maria.

"Pleased to meet you," I began, when she finally released my hand. "Do you have a first aid kit in here somewhere? I need to fix up that cut," I said as I jutted my chin at Dylan.

Maria nodded. "Yeah we do. It's out through the back in the employee break room. Dylan will show you where it is." Maria turned to Dylan and reached up to carefully angle his cut cheek for a better look. "It's deep, gonna have to clean that right up."

Maria then slipped the kitchen towel off of Dylan's shoulder, and flipped it over her own. "I'll watch the bar, you two go on through."

As Dylan led the way out through the side door, Maria called out just before I ducked my head through the doorway. "I wasn't kidding about the job, by the way. It's yours if you want it."

Chapter 6

DYLAN

"Give me those," James sighed, gently grasping the band aids and swabs from my hands. "Just sit on the table," he ordered.

And I did as I was told.

James and I were both in the break room, with the first aid kit open on the table. And there was a confusing array of plasters, solutions and bandages scattered across the table top.

The break room was tiny, even smaller than my first room at college (which was saying something). And there was barely enough room for the two-person table in the middle.

The beige and green decor of the break room was drab. And, it was a left over design choice from the previous owner of the bar.

When the bar was busy, late in the evening, there was rarely any time to come back here. But, even then, this space was so dreary, I preferred to take my breaks outside.

And yet, being in here in this cramped space, so close to James, I didn't want to be anywhere else in the world right now. Which was a thought that was starting to trouble me.

'Be cool, this is just a man crush, you've had these before.' I reminded myself. And it was the truth.

I wasn't ashamed to admit I knew a good looking guy when I saw one. But James also had a magnetism to him, a quiet strength that I liked being around. And I'd only known him for a day.

I watched as James busied himself with the items in the first aid kit. He looked like he knew his way around this stuff, certainly much better than me. My personal first aid knowledge went as far as knowing what a band-aid was, and knowing that ointment hurt like a son of a gun.

Which was why I began to eye James warily, when he grabbed both the ointment and a cotton swab.

"This first aid kit is pretty well stocked," James said, his voice colored with appreciation.

"Should be," I said, shifting in my seat as I kept my wary gaze on the ointment bottle, "since that wasn't the first time someone didn't appreciate being cut off."

James paused mid-movement, the concern in his eyes pinning me in place. "That isn't the first time Mack has punched you?"

I shook my head. "It's the first time he's tried. He's a sullen drunk, but he's never come at me like that."

James hummed thoughtfully, as he returned to fix my cheek. I winced, swallowing the pain back as the ointment seared my wound. "It only stings a little," James chuckled, "and you're acting like you've just been shot."

"Oh yeah? Well, that'd probably hurt less than this," I mumbled, my voice growing close to sounding petulant.

Thankfully, the ointment application was brief. And James moved in closer to apply a touch of petroleum jelly to my cheek, followed by a couple of band-aids.

As he worked, I could feel the radiating heat of his body, what with him stood so close. And his surprisingly fresh cologne was subtle, as his musk filled my senses.

"I might take her up on her offer," James startled me out of my silent sniffing—*yes, honest to goodness sniffing*—of his cologne.

"Huh, you... what?"

James grasped my chin, turning my head to the side to admire his work. "That should do it," he said with a nod, as he continued. "I might take up Maria's offer of a job, and do a few security shifts here at the bar, after work."

I raised an eyebrow. "You've worked security before?"

James mouth quirked, "nope. But, I figure I could just loom around the doorway, intimidating people who look like they're getting out of hand."

I returned his half smile with one of my own, as I stood up. Straightening, I took half a step back. I needed to put a little bit of space between myself and James, before I went and did something stupid. "Well, the pay isn't great, but you can get all the free stale peanuts you can eat."

James laughed, a deep sound that felt good to hear. "Hey, I'd happily work for free," James told me, as he moved to sit on the table where I'd just sat. The movement closed the distance I'd put between us. And in this small room, that left me with my back almost against the wall.

"You would?"

"Sure, I'd be happy to help you keep homophobic guys like that Mack fella out of this place."

I paused. "Wait, you think Mack's homophobic?"

"Yup," James said solemnly, with a sigh. "He's never gotten in your face before now, right?"

I nodded.

"And then he came out with that whole *'boyfriends'* line, earlier." James sighed, "I've dealt with guys like that before. I've been openly bi for years, and one or two guys at the station I used to work at, didn't take well to that."

I just about managed to keep my jaw from dropping, and tried to look nonplussed at the news that James was bisexual.

I mean, I didn't have a problem with it. Hell, I've even thought about it more than once, although that was all in my long forgotten past.

The tension in the room had gone up a notch. And I could feel my manhood begin to harden, pushing up against the fabric of my briefs, desperate to be touched.

It was like it had a mind of its own. Then again, taking in James chiseled jawline, broad shoulders, and his amazing cobalt eyes, I couldn't blame my dick for springing to life.

I let my imagination run away with me, my breath becoming a little more rapid, as a single thought soon blossomed into a vivid depiction of me humping James handsome face.

But, I'm straight! Have been straight my entire 23 years. That doesn't just change in a day.

"Caught you by surprise with that one, huh?" James stated, shaking me from my wet daydream. Although, his confident smile was belied by a touch of apprehension creasing the corners of his eyes.

I shook my head. "No, no, um, I'm cool with it," I began, mentally wincing at my weak denial. I reached up to rub my face, momentarily forgetting about my cut cheek long enough to touch it. Pain flared up again and I hissed at the sting.

James indicated at my cheek. "You really need to leave it alone, try not to touch it."

"Yup, yup," I immediately agreed, dropping my hand away from my face. And with nothing to occupy my hands, I tucked them into my jeans pocket. "I was simply a little surprised."

"Really?" James asked, his head cocked. He looked at me curiously. "I thought you knew..." he swung a pointed finger between us, "...and well, with the way you've been flirting with me this whole time."

I blanched. "Wait, what? Flirting?" I snatched my hands out of my jeans pocket, and crossed my arms. "I'm not gay. I'm not even interested in any of that," I lied.

Chapter 7

JAMES

My heart dropped to my stomach.

I was so sure I was picking up the signals, getting all of the right signs, those little things that let you know a guy is playing on the same team as you. But, seems like I'd been out of the game for so long, my gaydar was broken beyond repair.

It had felt good to feel wanted...even in the brief time that I'd known Dylan. And my ever-present awareness of the scars on my neck had disappeared when I was around him. I felt comfortable around him, and I thought he felt the same way too.

'Well, that was fun while it lasted,' I thought to myself, hating how that idea soured my mood.

I stood up abruptly, and out of the corner of my eye, I saw how that startled Dylan. And it stung to see him lean away from me, as though he were disgusted.

I busied myself with putting the first aid kit back in order. "Anyway, gotta get back to the shop," I said, keeping my eyes averted as I repacked everything as fast as I could.

"Woah, wait," Dylan said, stepping forward to place a hand on my shoulder. "Is that it?"

I stopped repacking, pausing to look at him. "What do you mean?"

Dylan stopped, his eyebrows raised high. He tugged on my shoulder, turning me to face him. "I didn't mean it like that, that came out harsher than I meant. I just meant that I've never...like I've never thought about...at least not with hot guys or anything..."

"So, what did you mean?" I pressed again. And then my mind caught up with what Dylan had said. "You think I'm hot?"

"Sure, I mean, look at you. You're really well built, way more than me," Dylan had started to ramble, scratching the back of his head sheepishly, in a way that I was beginning to find adorable. "So, yeah, if I had to do a guy, you'd be it," Dylan said with a helpless shrug.

So, I'd read the signs right after all. It had been a while since I'd been bold enough to make a move on someone, especially as I let my self-doubt hold me back.

But not now, not anymore. I wanted this guy, wanted to take him right on the break room table, wanted to feel him clench with pleasure around my cock.

And, as I let my eyes travel down Dylan's body, I saw a distinct delicious shape stretching his jeans, letting me know that he wanted me too.

I moved forward, first aid kit forgotten, as I stepped into Dylan's personal space. And, to his credit, he didn't back away.

"If you had to do a guy, huh," I began, dropping my voice low, "sounds like you've thought about it a lot." I then dipped my head, reaching up to rest a hand on the wall behind the blond man. "And when you've thought about it, what did you imagine me doing to you?"

Dylan's face flushed, his breathing shallow as we stood with barely a fingers-width separating us.

"I don't know," Dylan hesitated, but he never dropped his aroused gaze from mine, "mostly just how it would feel to have your lips on my..." his voice trailed away.

"On your, what? Lips?" I let my gaze drop from his eyes down to his lips as Dylan swiped a tongue to wet them. "Or, around your..." this time I let my voice trail off, raising my eyes to meet his meaningfully. With that, I pinned him with a stare filled with a sensual promise.

My cock was rock hard now, stretching my pants so noticeably, that if Dylan took a sneaky look, he'd know exactly what I was promising to give him.

The pause was long, stretching forever, and yet probably only lasted a handful of seconds. And then...

"Fuck it," Dylan said, as he reached up to grab the back of my head, and pulled my mouth to his.

Chapter 8

DYLAN

I was kissing a man. Oh shit!

Still, my surprise at my brazen move, didn't stop me mid-kiss. Instead, it only made me kiss James even harder, as our tongues battled.

At first, the kiss got sloppy as our mouths fought. But then I held back, letting James take the lead and push his sweet tongue deep into my mouth.

We kissed for long minutes, my arms looped around his neck, as we breathed each other in. My breath deepened as James pressed his body against mine.

James height advantage meant that his firm member pressed hard against my lower abdomen. And I couldn't resist pressing my own cock up against his firm body in return.

Finally, we released each other, and James leaned back to peer down at me.

His searching gaze held a look of concern, as though he wasn't sure I wanted this. Screw that, I wanted this more than I ever would have thought.

"We should lock the door."

"Huh?" James asked confused.

"For privacy," I continued with a small shrug, "Maria said we could take our time back here, but I'd still rather not take the chance of her catching us."

James smiled at that. "Catching us doing what, exactly? Kissing?" James took half a step back, as he gave me room to lock the door.

Once I heard the lock 'click' into place, I returned to move in front of James, this time with my back to the door. "I don't want her catching us doing the things I imagined you doing to my dick."

James let loose a slow chuckle as I unbuckled my jeans, letting them drop to the floor carelessly, before reaching inside my briefs to free my cock.

Needing no more prompting from me, James immediately dropped to his knees, reaching up to tug my briefs down a little more, so that even my neatly trimmed balls were free from the fabric of my underwear.

I was so hard that my cock twitched when James warm breath merely caressed it. I'd never felt so fucking aroused in my life.

But, James didn't give me what I wanted, what I needed. At least not yet. Instead, he began kissing my washboard abs, laying a trail of warm caresses all around them.

I resisted the urge to grab the back of his head, and simply guide his mouth right where I needed it to be.

So, to keep myself from going straight into it, I raised my hands and placed them behind my head, keeping my gaze down as I watched James explore my body with his mouth.

Soon enough, he reached my cock, his mouth now inches away from the tip of my dick. I thrust forward—I couldn't help myself—but James deftly moved his head back enough to keep my cock at bay.

"Now, now," James chuckled, "you're eager, aren't you."

"Fuck, yes, please," I whined, letting my hands drop from my head to my sides. My fingers twitched as I strained to stop myself from grabbing his head. "I need you to put it in your mouth now...*fuck*!"

Before I'd even had a chance to finish my sentence, James slipped his lips around my cock, sliding my entire shaft into his mouth.

I gasped, rocking back with pleasure as he swallowed me whole.

He hummed, and it was a deep delicious sound, one that sent charged thrills from the tip of my cock to the bottom of my balls.

James head bobbed up and down as he worked me over, his mouth slick over my manhood. He'd also now placed his large palms on my ass, grabbing a firm handful of each cheek, steadying me as I pressed myself into him.

I was lost to the feel of it, as my hips thrust ever harder in time with James.

When he pulled back, I pulled back. And when he thrust forward, so did I.

Reaching down, I placed both hands on the back of his head as he pleasured me, and gave me the best fucking blow job I'd ever had in my life.

"God, that's it," I whispered, as James took me so deep in his mouth, I could feel my cock head brush the back of his throat. "Don't stop, don't stop, I'm getting so close," I urged him.

My words came out rushed, my grunts now beginning to blend in with James humming—and even growls—as I thrust hard into his face.

I could feel my balls begin to swing, pitching high enough with each thrust, that they repeatedly slapped James on his chin.

It was all too much. And my cock was now so sensitive, I had to let him know before I blew!

"I'm gonna come," I gasped, my head rocking back as my eyes cast toward the ceiling. And I was consumed by the all encompassing tension as my body started to explode. "I'm coming, I'm coming, I'M COMING!" I said with a strangled scream, as with one final thrust, I released every drop of my hot need deep into James throat.

And to my surprise, James swallowed it all.

Chapter 9

JAMES

It took a long moment after his salty release, but soon enough, I felt Dylan's cock begin to soften in my mouth.

So I let Dylan's dick slip slowly from my lips, flicking my tongue off the end of his hypersensitive tip. It was a move that made Dylan's butt cheeks clench tight in my hands as he hissed.

"Holy fuck," Dylan gasped, as I reveled in the taste of him, swallowing his cum. I slid my hands from his butt cheeks, to reach up to grasp the hands he'd place behind my head.

Looking up, I saw that Dylan's eyes were still closed, a broad smile of pleasure on his lips. And it felt good to be the one who put that smile on his face.

I brought the palm of one of his hands to my lips and kissed it, as I continued to kneel in front of him. This drew Dylan's attention to me, his green eyes gazing down in amazement. "That was fucking incredible."

I nodded. "You're welcome," I replied as I rose up from the floor, standing in front of him. I gently grabbed his face, pulling him into an intense kiss, as I slid my tongue back into his mouth. I put everything into the embrace, letting him know through my caressing tongue, how much I wanted him.

I was so hard now. My cock painfully pulsated as I pressed myself flush against Dylan. Finally, after long moments, I leaned back, letting us both gasp for air.

"I can taste my cum in your mouth," Dylan said with a low chuckle, as he began to fumble at my belt buckle, "but I really want to taste yours instead."

I let him work at the leather belt, pulling the loop free, so that he could unzip my jeans. My eyes drifted down his body, before settling on the pants and briefs that were still pooled around Dylan's ankles.

"You want to pull up your pants first? Or are you just gonna drop to you knees?" Dylan paused, stopping just as his finger tips reached my zipper.

He looked down at himself, shrugged, then looked up at me. "I can sort that later," he answered, before dropping to the floor in front of me.

I grinned, as Dylan finished unzipping me and reached in to my briefs to pull out my hard firm dick. I carefully watched Dylan's expression, knowing that this was going to be the first time he'd ever taken a dick in his mouth. I needed to be sure he wanted this.

So, I was unsure what to do when a look of surprised apprehension appeared on Dylan's face. Before I could voice a question, Dylan spoke.

"You're fucking huge!" Dylan said, looking up at me, eyes wide. "I'm going to gag on your cock, if I take it in as deep as you did mine."

"You don't have to..." I began, but Dylan rushed on.

"No, I want to," Dylan quickly answered, waving my assurances away.

I nodded. But, Dylan's mouth wasn't the hole I wanted to pound my dick into.

"What?" Dylan asked, in a way that made me realize that I'd just voiced my last thought out loud. *Fuck.*

Well, in for a penny, in for a...

"You don't need to swallow me," I said as I reached out a hand to bring Dylan to his feet. I looped my arms around him, bringing him in close, as my firm cock pressed between our two hard bodies. "If you want to take me all the way in, let me take you from behind."

"I've never done anal before...giving or getting," Dylan replied, as I dipped my head down to whisper into his ear.

"Don't worry, I know what I'm doing."

Chapter 10

DYLAN

'*H*oly shit, this is happening.' I thought to myself.

The moment I'd shakily nodded my head '*Yes*' at letting James take me in the ass, he quickly got to work.

I could tell by the thick long hardness of him, that he was eager to plow me, but I tried to hide my nervousness...or was it nervous curiosity?

When I first pulled James cock out, it took my breath away. Firstly, because his dick was nearly twice the length of my own. And secondly, because I knew that if he face-fucked me with that thing, it certainly would take my breath away by choking me.

So why on earth did I think I was going to be able to fit it all in my ass?

Still, I was going to soon find out how deeply I could take his cock, since I was now face down, and spread out over the break room table.

Grabbing the petroleum jelly from the first aid kit, James had then cleared the table top, before telling me to lay down over it.

It left me standing at an uncomfortable angle, my puckered asshole now free and clear for James to enter.

James stood right behind me. "Okay, I'm just smearing some on now," he said, giving me fair warning.

My hands clenched the edge of the table as James smeared the lube around my hole. The cool jelly contrasted with the heat of James fingers as he spread it around my entrance.

He worked in silence. And I swear he must have put nearly half a jar of the stuff onto my asshole before I finally spoke up. The anticipation was killing me. I turned around to look over my shoulder at him. "You gonna get started soon?"

James let loose a short bark of a laugh. "Just getting you nice and ready for me," he said as he then placed a small kiss on my hip. "This is your first time, remember?"

I nodded, turning back to face forward, and tried to relax my puckering hole. Soon enough, the wait was over, as I felt James slowly push a finger into me.

I moaned at the pleasurable burn of it. I couldn't help it. I'd never fingered myself before, or been fingered, but this wasn't what I imagined it would feel like.

James slid his finger in and out a few times, adding what felt like more jelly each time he penetrated me.

"Okay, lets try a couple fingers now," James said.

"Yes," I hissed when I felt two fingers slide in. One finger felt good, but two fingers made me squirm. I focused on relaxing again, spreading my legs a little further apart to keep me steady.

"Still good?" James asked.

"Yeah," I answered quickly, my voice low, "keep going."

When James pushed his third finger in, that is when I felt my asshole stretch to accommodate him. I closed my eyes to luxuriate in the burn of it, as James bent his fingers to search my inner walls.

I grunted, and my balls jumped, when I felt him rub a particular section of the inside of my hole. He was stimulating what must have been my prostate.

The male G-spot...or so I've read.

"God, that feels good," I said, the words falling from my lips as I clenched my eyes tight to enjoy how his fingertips manipulated my spot.

"Guess you're ready then," James said. I opened my eyes and looked over my shoulder to find him positioning the tip of his hard cock where his fingers had just been.

Slowly, *so very slowly*, James inched his rock hard manhood into my tight lubed ass. And inch by slippery inch, I moaned as he entered me.

He kept going, and going, and going. And just when I was feeling so full, so incredibly stuffed, Jame stopped. His cock was finally in me, all the way, and balls deep.

And my god, it felt amazing!

James then reached up to place a bracing hand on my shoulder, as he slowly pulled out. And I reveled in the feel of his cock stroking against the entire length of my inner walls.

But, just before he slipped completely out of me, I felt James thrust back in, firmer and harder this time. And I let loose a grunt that was almost as loud as the moan that left James lips.

"God, you feel so good," James told me, his voice tight, as he began to slowly fuck me. His grip on my shoulder tightened as he thrust into me again, and again. His other hand, grasped my hip to hold me steady as he moved.

It wasn't long before his thrusts became so urgent, we began to shift the table. And the table legs scratched rhythmically against the floor, as James pushed himself into my ass. Plus, it was all I could do to hang onto the table edge, as James took me.

I knew we were now both moaning and grunting so loud, there was a strong chance we'd be heard back inside the bar, but I didn't care.

James grunts got lower, more gravelly, as he leaned forward, his weight pressing on my back. His long slow thrusts had now become short hard pounds.

"Ugh, ugh, ugh..." James grunted, and I clenched my asshole, trying to make myself as tight as possible for him.

"I'm coming, I'm coming, I'm coming..." James refrained, before he pressed his mouth flush against my back, as though he were using my shoulder to mute his carnal moans.

Chapter 11

JAMES

I exploded with hot need.

Everything I had blew out of me, all with one final hard thigh-slapping thrust. And, with a muffled cry into Dylan's shoulder, I tried to bury my moan of joy into the firm muscles of his back, as I emptied my cum into him.

We remained like that for a long moment, my forehead resting on Dylan's back, nothing but the sounds of our heavy breathing filling the room.

When I eventually raised my head, I noticed Dylan had turned to peer at me over his shoulder. "You good?" Dylan asked. And I could hear a hint of insecurity coloring his voice.

I quickly put a stop to all doubts in his mind, and dipped my head to kiss him. While Dylan twisted awkwardly at an angle so that I could capture his lips, putting everything I had into our passionate lock.

I moaned as I felt Dylan clench his butt hole a couple times, as though he were trying to milk every last drop of cum from my still deliciously sensitive cock head. I shivered, enjoying the thrill of it, before I finally released his lips and slid my dick out of his ass. "That was perfect," I said as I caught my breath.

Righting myself, I shuffled a few steps back, giving Dylan the room to straighten himself up off the table. "What about you? Are you good?" I returned Dylan's question, as we both set about pulling up our pants, and fixing our clothes.

I felt a connection to this man, an electricity that began from the moment he'd turned up at the garage. The last thing I wanted was to scare Dylan away, especially after our mind-blowing fuck.

I wanted—*needed*—more from him. I'd taken Dylan for the first time, and I wasn't prepared for it to be the last.

Dylan nodded. "Yeah, I mean, I'm a little sore," he said with a chuckle as he tucked his shirt back into his jeans.

I decided to test the waters, trying to feel things out, moving towards him as though he were a wild animal about to bolt off.

But too my surprise, Dylan welcomed the arms I wrapped around him, and he fell into my embrace.

With his head nestled in the crook of my shoulder, we stood flush as Dylan nuzzled my neck. And it took me a second to remember that the flesh on my neck—that Dylan was pressing warm lips against—were my burn scars.

I stiffened, remembering that the scars were there all over again. My time with Dylan had managed to do something that I'd been struggling to do for a long while.

Being with Dylan made me forget that those scars were even there.

Chapter 12

DYLAN

I felt James become rigid, the moment I placed a soft kiss on his marks. I knew he felt self-conscious about them. The way he'd hid his face behind his hoodie, when I met him, was testament to that.

But, I didn't care about them. I like this guy—more than liked him—and I felt a connection to him I'd never felt with anyone.

So, I did the one thing I'd been wanting to do since he'd arrived in the bar. I kissed his scars to let him know I wanted all of him.

'Dang it,' I thought to myself. *'Great move Dylan, you've made him feel even more self-conscious about them now'.*

Leaning back, I peered up a few inches to find James looking down at me. Yet there was no look of anger or shame in his eyes. Simply a look of curiosity.

I stroked my hand up and down his back. "I've been meaning to ask you how you got them," I began, and pressed forward, ignoring James slight *'no'* shake of his head. "But you can tell me about it some time. For now," I paused to plant a small kiss on James lips, "lets get back into the bar, before Maria comes looking for us."

James nodded silently. And then, as we both loosened our hold on one another, I noticed a cocky smile begin to spread across his face. "So, there's going to be a next time?"

EPILOGUE

JAMES

"This thing has maybe another month left in it. It was the best I could do," I said helplessly.

It had been nearly a month since our tryst at the bar. The first of many. I'd become somewhat of a regular at Dylan's place of work. *And at his apartment. And in his bed.*

Yet, this was the first time Dylan had been back to my place of work, since he'd dropped off his old beat-up car.

Inside the garage, I listened to the car hum its dilapidated thrum, as Dylan revved the engine of his vehicle. "So, what you're telling me," he said, after switching off the engine and getting out of his car to stand beside me, "is that it'll die on me the moment I drive it out of here."

He looked forlornly at his car, and I couldn't help but move to wrap an arm around his shoulders. Resting a chin on his head, I answered, "pretty much, but it's amazing it lasted this long." I indicated at the bonnet of the car. "Some parts of it's engine are genuine antiques. You'd probably get more out of it by taking it apart for scrap."

Dylan looped an arm around my waist, his warm palm coming to rest on my hip. He snuck his finger tips up under the thin fabric of my short-sleeved teeshirt, and brushed them against my skin.

"Well, the babe magnet served me well. Even did its best work with its final hurrah."

I gave Dylan a questioning look. "It did?"

"Yes," Dylan replied. "On its very last legs, it brought me to you." Dylan reached up to cup my face—no longer hidden behind the hoodies I used to wear—and brought me in for a quick kiss on the cheek.

But, that wasn't enough for me.

I cast around a quick look to check if Tony was around, or if any customers had wandered in. Seeing that we were still alone, I lightly grasped Dylan's chin.

I then claimed his lips with my own, my tongue sliding into his hot wet mouth, as I made him mine all over again.

THE END

Thank you so much for reading Hard Hart!

The next book in the 'First Time for Everything' series is available for purchase right now: https://books2read.com/u/b5WO96

Or you can simply keep reading for a quick sneak peak into 'Hard Case'...

Hard Case

A Straight To Gay Bi Awakening Steamy MM Short Story
(First Time for Everything Series)
By B.T. Haiyes

Chapter 1

CASE

"Alright, Everyone gather round! Come on, I know you can all hear me, lets group up!"

I cringed, slowly turning to face Evan, as the man bellowed for everyone's attention.

"Yes, Casey, even you too!"

This time I made no effort to hide my annoyance, as Evan singled me out of the group.

"OK, now that I have all your attention," Evan continued, ignoring the low groans and mutters of my co-workers. "I just want to say that I really appreciate that you're all here. And we are all going to have a great time!" Evan's voice up-ticked with forced enthusiasm, reminding me of an aerobics instructor inspiring a club of gym-goers.

A group of twenty or so of us were crammed into the summer-camp styled eating area. And the log cabin cafeteria had a few long wooden tables, with rustic benches set either side of each table.

I shifted around on the hard wooden bench, as I folded my arms. And what little hope I had for getting through this mandatory team building weekend, quietly drained away.

I was not designed for the great outdoors. I liked to do my exercising indoors, in well air-conditioned bug-free gyms. Ideally one with a WI-FI connection and other civilized amenities.

But, none of those things where available here in this log cabin village nestled deep in a forest.

'There are horror movies written about this kind of place,' I thought to myself.

As Evan began what I could tell was an over-rehearsed speech about teamwork, I felt someone gently bump my shoulder.

Turning, I found Janet sidling up, moving to take up the empty seat beside me. I smiled as I took in her lightly flushed cheeks, and her blond hair pulled back into a tight ponytail.

My cubicle neighbor—or cubicle cellmate as Janet liked to call it—was one of the few people I felt comfortable chatting with at work. And she was cute too. But, something always held me back from taking the plunge and asking her out on a date.

"God," Janet whispered, just low enough to be heard by me alone, "he's going to be like this all weekend isn't he," she continued, jutting a chin at the wildly gesticulating Evan.

I rubbed my chin thoughtfully. "Maybe a bear will eat him, and we can go back home early."

Janet snorted at that, drawing the attention of Evan who paused mid-speech.

"Excuse me, guys?" Evan waved his clipboard in our direction. "We need to stay on track here. Got a lot on the itinerary today."

A chorus of groans rose from around the room.

"Look," Evan sighed, as he took in the twenty person sales team. "I don't want to pull rank, but I'm the boss here."

"No, you're not!" One of our group yelled out, their voice clear over everyone else's low chatter.

And, they were absolutely right.

Evan was just another sales subordinate, like the rest of us. The only reason he was even heading the team this weekend was because he volunteered. Our boss had asked if someone could take over leading this weekend retreat, and Evan had jumped at the chance.

Still, it made sense Evan would volunteer, as this whole thing was his idea in the first place.

A few months back, the company sent out a memo asking for team building suggestions. And during one of our weekly sales meetings, the topic of the memo came up.

I suggested giving us a pay rise. While, Evan suggested a one-off outdoor team building weekend.

And Evan's stupid idea won out.

Still, it turns out that even our esteemed boss didn't want to muddy his expensive shoes humping up hillsides.

So, of course, our boss did what all great bosses do. He passed the buck — *sorry, I mean delegated* — to someone else.

And, unfortunately, that buck was picked up by Evan...who was a man who thought that 6am was a Saturday morning lie-in.

"Okay, okay. Settle down," Evan waved away the complaints. "I know some of you didn't want to be here," Evan said, giving me a pointed frown.

It was a look I did not appreciate, and I mimed my own mocking look of surprise. Although I barely managed to keep myself from giving Evan the finger as well.

I'd made no secret about the fact that I too wanted to duck out of this weekend. As had many of my co-workers. But, the company emphasized that we would all be evaluated on our level of participation this weekend.

"Regardless," Evan continued, giving me a half-raised brow in warning, "we are going to have a great time, because we are all being guided this weekend by..." Evan then tucked his clipboard underneath one arm, and crouched to do a thigh-slapping drum roll.

I didn't hold back my eye-roll at Evan's theatrics, but my curiosity peeked when Evan straightened up to indicate off to the side.

"Benjamin!" Evan declared, and I started when I noticed a man stood in the corner, leaning against the wall.

I didn't recognize him from work. And I certainly hadn't noticed when he'd entered the room.

"Who is he?" Janet whispered, and I shrugged with a helpless shake of my head. "Did you even see him come in here," Janet asked with a look of curiosity that matched my own.

"Nope," I answered, as I watched Benjamin move to the front of the room. And as he did, I got a better look at him.

And, my God, how did I not notice him earlier!

This guy was tall, and broad with it too. His black fitted short-sleeve teeshirt stretched over his huge traps and impossibly broad shoulders. And his biceps where all taut muscle, as he eased to a standstill at the front of the room.

I'd always felt self-conscious about my 5'9" frame. And I knew Evan stood at around 5'11" — a fact that he liked to frequently point out to me.

However, Benjamin easily stood over half a foot taller than Evan.

Yet, as impressive as his body was, it was Benjamin's eyes that grabbed my attention. Those deep hazel orbs calmly scanned the room.

And once Benjamin's gaze drifted over to meet my own, I could feel a blush begin from the base of my neck, crawling its way up to my cheeks. I held the large man's attention for a moment, before he broke off our stare to take in the others.

"Wow," Janet's whisper startled me. I'd forgotten she was there. "He is so hot," Janet said, all but moaning out the words. "I would totally do him. I'd climb that man like a tree."

I began to nod in agreement, before catching myself.

'Get it together,' I silently scolded myself, pointedly ignoring the peculiar look Janet turned my way.

This wasn't the first time I'd caught myself slipping in my appreciation of a good looking man. But, there's nothing wrong in appreciating beauty, in all of its forms. Right?

That doesn't mean I'm gay, it just means I have a good eye. *Right?*

"Yes, well..." Evan began awkwardly, drawing my own (and everyone else's) attention back his way.

From the look on his face, it seemed as though Evan thought Benjamin would jump at the chance to introduce himself to the group. Instead, Benjamin stood silently, looking as though he were more than done with Evan's theatrics. "Anyway, this is Benjamin," Evan continued, turning back to the group, "and he will be leading us on our first team building exercise..."

"Ben."

My mouth quirked into a small smile when Benjamin — or rather Ben — neatly interrupted Evan. Ben's voice was rich and deep, his singular word carrying authority.

'And it seems like he's a man of few words as well,' I thought to myself.

Meanwhile, Evan turned a look of surprise over at Ben. "I'm sorry?"

Ben stared down — way down — to look Evan in the eye. "My name's Ben. Benjamin is my father," he replied, his answer concise and to the point.

The quirk on my lips broadened into a grin when I noticed how intimidated Evan was by Ben.

"Of course," Evan said hesitantly, before clearing his throat with a brief nod. "Yes, well, Ben here is our guide for the weekend. He has years of knowledge about the forest around us. He even grew up around here, isn't that right Ben?" Evan asked him.

Ben said nothing.

Evan cleared his throat again before plowing on, pointedly turning his attention onto his clip board. "And first thing on the team building menu, is a seven mile hike on the Teriann Trail beside this village."

"Seven miles! Seriously!? You can't be serious!" Janet said, loud enough to make me cringe as she yelled out in surprise, right beside my ear.

A few of us in the room — myself included — let loose a few noises of agreement with Janet.

I spoke up, backing her up. "Come on Evan," I began, as I made a show of glancing at my watch. "Seven miles at 6:15am? We haven't even had breakfast yet."

"Breakfast comes after hiking." The reply didn't come from Evan. Instead, Ben had moved half a step forward, pinning me with the most intimidating glare I'd ever seen in my life. It was even more intimidating than the one my former soccer coach gave me, when he said he'd never known anyone less athletic than me.

The memory of my coach calling me out in front of my high school gym class stung a little.

But, Ben's glare did something altogether different to me. Instead, his eyes seemed to send a flash of heat through my body that felt nothing like shame or embarrassment.

"The fresh air will do you all good." Ben told us, his words holding a sense of finality on the subject.

Chapter 2

BEN

'This is the most annoying bunch of moaning city dwellers that I've ever dealt with,' I thought to myself.

From the moment I'd led this gang of corporate suits to the trail, they'd started to complain.

Everything — literally *every* darned thing — was apparently too much for them.

Too much bugs this, and too much walking that. And *'my feet hurt'* this, and *'is that a bear?'* that.

'Did any of them read the damn brochure before they came out here?'

Luckily, my job today was to simply guide the group through the forest this morning. And, with any luck, this task would be done within a couple hours.

'That's if I'm able to keep them moving, and we're not stuck out here come nightfall.'

Thankfully, Margaret and Steve, (the owners of this whole cabin getaway), would be dealing with this whiny lot the rest of the weekend.

I was only here to make sure no one wandered off in the night, and got lost in the nearby forest.

And the forest was looking particularly beautiful this morning. Crisp morning sun-rays splintered through the impossibly green tall trees that lined our pathway.

The path was well trodden, (I'd walked it often enough myself), and there were local wildlife tracks all along it.

And I would have showed this group some of that wildlife, if they could have stayed quiet long enough to not scare the critters off.

"How many miles have we covered so far?" Evan sidled up to me, his hands clutching the sides of his waist, as a faint wheeze eased from him.

I bit back my criticism at the hefty backpack he insisted on bringing on this walk. What it was filled with, God only knows. Yet, what I did know was that the bag was heavy enough to leave Evan winded by the end of the first mile.

"About three or four miles. We're already past the half way mark," I answered, indicating the path ahead of us, "we should be looping back around. We'll be back at the cabin village soon enough."

"Oh thank goodness," I heard Evan whisper to himself, before turning around to speak to the group. "We're half way there, guys!" Evan said loudly, his arm waving around as he drew a loop in the air, "we should be looping back around, and be right back at the village in no time at all." Evan repeated my answer almost verbatim.

"Yeah, we know," a voice commented from somewhere behind me in the crowd. "Ben just said that. We're tired, Evan, not deaf."

I held back a chuckle and peered over my shoulder to find out who the commentator was. That's when I noticed the speaker from back at the cabin meet and greet — Casey was it? — jogging towards me.

He didn't seem winded like the others in the group. *Looks like he keeps himself fit enough,* I thought, mentally nodding at him in silent appreciation.

"We need a bit of a break," Casey pointed a thumb over his shoulder at the other hikers behind him.

Casey didn't seem like he needed a breather, but I shrugged. I had to admit, I had been keeping a fast pace. I wanted to get the hike done quickly, so I could get away from all the grumbling.

I nodded. "Fair enough, Casey," I said and then addressed the group. "Let's take a break. Drink some water, stretch a bit, and will get back to it in ten minutes. And don't wander off."

Mutters of ascent rose up from my not-so-merry band of hikers. And some of them collapsed to the floor, as though they'd just run a half-marathon.

I ruefully shook my head, and out of the corner of my eye, I caught Case staring at me.

When he noticed he'd been caught, I watched as a curious glance of something — I don't know what — flash across his features. But, it was quickly replaced with clear embarrassment.

"Yes? Is there anything else?"

Casey sheepishly rubbed his chin. "It's Case, by the way," Case answered, as I continued to gaze at him with interest. "Evan has a bit of a problem with nicknames, finds them too informal so he claims. But people call me Case."

I nodded at the rambling, filing away the information for later. I could feel something, a hint of tension maybe, pass between Case and myself.

But, as soon as it came, it disappeared. And I mentally shrugged it off.

It'd been ages since I'd last had a man in my bed. And I wasn't about to get back on the dating wagon by hitting on the first straight guy that caught my eye.

Chapter 3

CASE

"Damn it, where the hell am I?" I groused, as I looked every which way to find nothing but trees and thickets.

I know I shouldn't have wandered off from the group. But, I'd been bursting to pee, and I didn't want an audience.

Besides, I also wanted to hide from Ben.

I hadn't meant to get caught staring, but I was inexplicably drawn by Ben's whole profile. From across a room, he was good looking. Yet, up close, Ben was damn-near an Adonis.

It was hard for me *not* to stare at him.

Still, I hadn't even meant to walk that far off. It was just a few steps — or a half dozen. But now I couldn't find that damned trail path again.

And I know Ben told us that there were no bears in these woods. But that's little comfort when your lost in the thickest part of a forest.

"Fuck!'" I yelled out, partly in frustration, partly in growing panic. Knowing my luck, I was probably going to die out here having been eaten by very aggressive beavers or something.

"Case?"

I halted, my body frozen by the hope that I'd heard someone say my name. "Hello?" I shouted out in reply.

"Case, it's Ben! Just keep talking, and I'll find you!"

Relief flooded my system. It filled me with a euphoric warmth that melted away all the tension and escalating panic I'd felt for the past half hour.

"Ben! I'm here!" I yelled, as I spun around in an attempt to spot him. I continued babbling loudly, "I'm over here. I got lost! I'm over here!"

"Yeah, I figured," Ben yelled back. His voice now sounded near enough that I could pinpoint his direction.

Peering through the trees, I found Ben making his way towards me. I waved at him, and he half-waved back.

"Your friend Janet said you'd gone missing," Ben told me as he neared, and I fought back the unmanly like urge to collapse with relief into his arms. "She said you'd gone to take a leak." Ben paused to look around the deep forest. "Not sure why you felt you had to walk off this far though."

"I know, I know. It was stupid of me to split off like that. But, you've found me now, so." I waved in the direction he'd come from, "shall we get back?"

"Yes, of course, Case. It was absolutely no problem finding you," Ben's voice was heavy with sarcasm. "No need to thank me."

I had the good grace to look sheepish at that. "Thanks. Seriously, thanks so much for finding me." I glanced around the woods. "I was sure I was gonna get eaten by beavers."

I was caught by surprise when Ben let loose a short laugh, a genuine honest to goodness sound of laughter, punctuated by a half smile.

"So, you *can* smile," I said, not bothering to hide my wide grin. "No, no, too late," I continued, as Ben fixed his face, returning to his more familiar scowl. "Way too late, I saw it. Now I'm going to tell everyone that you are actually capable of cracking a grin," I said with a laugh.

Ben rolled his eyes. "Let's get back," he said shortly before stomping off at my chuckles. Snapping a stern look over his shoulder, he tried to glare the smirk off my face.

It didn't work.

"Yep," I enjoyed his clear annoyance a little too much, "you're all warm and fuzzy." Trailing after him, I attempted to hop over a log in our path, but I misjudged the distance, and I caught my foot.

I already knew it was much too late to try and right myself, and I squeezed my eyes shut. Yet, as I prepared my face for impact, I felt Ben quickly slip his arms around my waist.

He had moved startlingly fast, fast enough to keep me upright. I, on the other hand, fell face first into Ben's broad chest, and our bodies now stood uncomfortably flush against one another.

My heart quickened when I leaned back to peer up at him. And I found his hazel orbs gazing right back at me.

We stayed like that for a long while, as I observed Ben's enlarged pupils. And it took me a few more moments to finally notice that a certain part of my body was also becoming enlarged.

In mortified panic, I rushed to get my feet under me. All the while, my shaft continued to thicken with excitement.

It was like it was reacting with a mind of its own, drawn by the heat radiating off Ben's body.

I took a couple of hurried steps back, keeping my eyes fixed to the ground, as I made a show of righting my clothes.

But I wanted the excuse of fussing with my jacket zipper, so that I could surreptitiously adjust my pants to hide my erection!

Thankfully, Ben said nothing while I fretted about with my clothes. Yet, once I finally dared to meet his gaze, I found him staring intently right back with a knowing look.

'Crap! Did he see me adjusting myself?' I thought with growing alarm.

I rushed to try and think of a plausible excuse to explain things away. But, when I opened my mouth to say something, Ben spoke first.

"Let's keep going, shall we?" And with that, Ben spun round to continue walking.

And, without another word, I meekly followed.

Chapter 4

BEN

It had been an interesting day so far.

After finally finding Case wandering around in a panic in the woods, I continued to lead the group along the remainder of the path.

The rest of the walk was without incident — and even all of the groups grumbling had seemed to subside a little bit too.

Along the walk, and all the way back to the cabins, I gave Case the odd look. Yet, not once did he return any of them.

It's been a while since I've had my gaydar ping for me as strongly as it did with Case. Particularly during that moment when I stopped him from falling over flat on his face.

As he'd stumbled away from me, Case had done a really bad job of hiding the way his hand drifted down to his crotch.

Still, I was surprised when I noticed it, because I for sure thought Case was straight. Yet, I know I felt something pass between Case and myself. There was no mistaking it. I know I felt an electricity.

'But did Case?' I questioned. *'Or am I simply projecting my own horniness?'*

A sliver of doubt clouded my memory of that moment with Case. Especially what with the way he studiously avoided looking my way (or meeting my eye) for the rest of the hike.

And to add insult to injury, Case had also flirted up a storm with some pony-tailed blond, on the remaining walk back to the cabins.

"WE WILL MEET OUR TARGETS THIS YEAR!"

The rising volume of chanting voices disrupted my thoughts. The grumbling hiking group from earlier — along with Case — were all inside the communal cabin behind me.

Stood out front on the decking, I listened to them, as I polished the apple I held against my shirt. And as I gazed up at the early evening sky, I shook my head at what I heard.

Margaret was apparently leading the group through what she had once told me was, 'an inner motivational gathering of outer souls'.

I had no clue what she meant, but I didn't hesitate to turn down the offer of joining the group for an evening of team building.

The smell of burnt sage wafted thickly out the cabins half-open window, as the voices continued to loudly refrain slogans.

This particular *motivational gathering* involved refraining statements such as, 'We Are Powerful Beings,' 'Let My Heart Serve My Mind' — and my personal favorite — 'Our Sales Targets, Our Rules!'.

I was pretty sure neither Margaret or Steve were clinical psychologists. So, I had a sneaky suspicion that their motivational sessions weren't exactly scientific.

Still, they paid me well. And they truly believed that what they did helped others. So, who was I to try and stand in their way.

The chanting behind me soon died down, replaced with a mixture of grumbles and cheers. And a few moments later, I heard the door of the cabin open up behind me, but I didn't bother to turn around.

I didn't need to. The voice that spoke up was one I was beginning to know very well.

"I need to go take a leak," Case said, speaking back to whomever. "I'll be right back as soon as possible."

"Okay, but hurry," I heard Margaret call out, "you'll miss the stick circle segment."

"Wouldn't miss it for the world," Case said, and I could hear the grimace in his voice as he closed the door, cutting off the noise inside the cabin.

The silence that followed was an awkward one, and lasted much too long. Long enough that I was almost tempted to turn around and face the man who seemingly stood stock still behind me.

Finally, Case broke the tension.

"Hey," Case said as he moved to stand beside me. I spared him a quick glance, giving him a wordless curt nod, before turning my gaze back towards the sky.

"Yeah well," Case voice trailed off when I said nothing.

If he wanted to try and fill the silence with small talk, he could go ahead. It was churlish of me, but I figured he was going to ignore me anyway. So, I saw no need to go out of my way to make conversation.

Case cleared his throat. "It looks to be shaping up to be a beautiful evening."

I grunted, taking another bite from my apple. I fully expected that to be the end of that, but it seemed Case was in no hurry to go anywhere.

"You got anymore of those?" Case asked, and that was enough to make me finally turn my head towards him.

I gave him a steady stare, unwilling to make myself vulnerable to a man I'd only met this morning.

I'd expected to see a smirk on his face, or some whimsical glance. Or maybe I expected him to continue to try and avoid my eye.

But, instead I was met by Case's own steady blue gaze, his eyes hopeful. So, I put him out of his misery and relented enough to answer.

"The kitchen is still open for at least another..." I glanced down at my watch, "...forty five minutes or so." I met his gaze once again. "They can whip you up something to eat, if you're hungry."

Case shook his head, rubbing the back of his neck, his eyes now turned down. "I'm not really hungry, or need a snack or anything ," Case rambled, and I tried not to find it endearing. "It's more that I saw you eating an apple. And I like apples. I mean, I've always thought I liked them. And then I thought, *'hey, maybe there are more apples'.* So I figured..."

I stopped his long-winded explanation with a wave of my hand. "Yup, I got it," I said, fighting to hold back a small smile.

Case blew out a breath, sounding frustrated as he rubbed a hand across his face. "Sorry about that. All the chanting in there has gotten to me. I just couldn't take another minute of all of that..." Case jutted a thumb towards the cabin window, the sounds of Margaret trying (and failing) to lead the group into another round of motivational shouts.

"It sounds like fun." I deadpanned, and Case laughed.

"I know you work here , but I can't wait to wrap this all up. I have no idea what soul massaging involves, but from what little I could pick up from Margaret, it definitely does not sound like my thing."

I nodded, sagely, "oh I don't know," I said, letting my cheeky side come through, "it depends on who is doing the massaging." And with that, I openly let my eyes roam all over Case's body.

To Be Continued...

To read the rest of 'Hard Case' you can find it right now here: https://books2read.com/u/b5WO96 [1]

ABOUT THE AUTHOR

Author B.T. Haiyes loves romance books, espresso and cheesecake — in no particular order.

Having started her freelance writing career back in 2015, she now carves out time in her work schedule, to write the kind of stories she loves to read.

Stories about men finding love in the most unlikely of places, are her particular favorites. Which is why she writes so much heartfelt MM insta-love short story fiction.

In her spare time — when she isn't writing or reading — she also likes to knit, cycle, and hike nearby trails.